My Tio's
PULSE

By Keith A. Newhouse

and the friends
of Pulse Orlando

Together we are strong. Together we are hope.

– Orlando United Assistance Center

My Tío's Pulse
By Keith A. Newhouse
Cover, Layout, and Art Direction by Ethan Long

AimHi Press and NCG Cares
Orlando, Florida
AimHiPress.com
©2018, Keith Newhouse

Names: Newhouse, Keith A.
Title: My Tío's Pulse / by Keith A. Newhouse
Description: Orlando, FL :AimHi Press, 2018. | Summary: When Angel learned how to take his pulse in gym class, he never imagined the effect that his newfound knowledge would have on his Uncle Luis...or the conversations that it would start.
Identifiers: LCCN 2018911464 (print) | ISBN 978-1-945493-11-9 (paperback)
Subjects: CYAC: Counseling. |Pulse. | Historical Events--Fiction. | Diversity—Fiction.
Classification: LCC PZ7.1.N49 My 2018 (print)
LC record available at https://lccn.loc.gov/2018911464

Why are you crying, Tío Luis?
When Angel learned how to take his pulse in gym class, he never imagined the effect that his newfound knowledge would have on his Uncle Luis...or the conversations that it would start.
Using expert language from Psychotherapist Kenny Tello, who worked directly with children and families affected by Pulse, My Tío's Pulse explains what happened at Pulse on June 12, 2016 in a clear and simple way that will give children the tools to talk about difficult topics and empower them to feel safe.

At school, I learned to measure my pulse.

A pulse means that my heart is beating and I am alive.

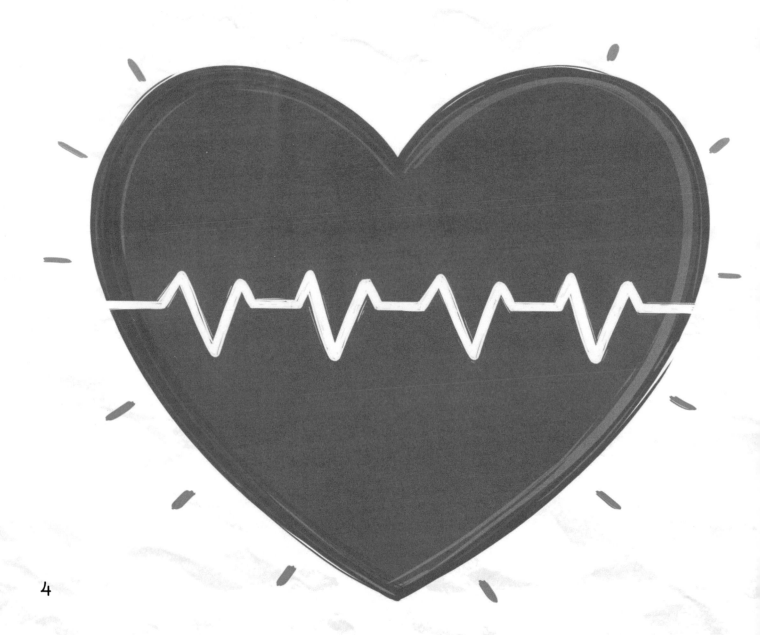

It's faster when I run . . .

and slower when I rest.

My pulse beats faster when I see my uncle, Tío Luis. He's Mama's "hermanito" or little brother.

When I told Tío Luis
about my pulse,
he became sad.

I asked Mama why.
She started to cry.

I asked Papa.
He said it was hard for
Mama to talk about.

I asked my teacher, Miss Morris.
She said that something happened that made
my uncle sad, but couldn't say more right now. 9

A few days later, Miss Morris announced a special guest coming to class.
I wondered who . . .

Miss Morris introduced Tío Luis and shared that he wanted to talk about something very important. Tío smiled and said, "Angel showed me that you've been learning to take your pulse."

13

"Pulse was also a place in Orlando, Florida where people went to dance and have fun. Everyone at Pulse was like my family."

"On June 12, 2016, an unsafe person who was angry came to Pulse and hurt many people. I was there."

16

Alice interrupted, "I remember! My Mom's friend made ribbons after it happened."

17

Tío Luis said, "Many were sad and those ribbons were one important way that people all over the world wanted to help. Everyone was praying and sending love to Orlando."

"Yes. I felt alone and confused. I kept my feelings inside me. I hardly left my room for weeks. I wondered if it was my fault."

Tío started to cry. I gave him a hug. "Gracias, Angel. I'm glad we are talking about this."

"Tío?" I asked. "Am I going to be hurt by an unsafe person?"

23

Miss Morris interrupted, "Although an unsafe person hurt people, we are safe. There are some things we can do to feel even more safe:

1. Talk about your feelings to feel better. Let others help when you feel sad or mad.

2. Always have an adult you trust. This could be a parent, relative, or teacher.

3. If there is something you don't understand, ask.

HOW TO FEEL SaFe:

1. Talk aBout your FEELINGS
2. Find a *TRUSTED* aDuLt.
3. ask Questions.

When Miss Morris finished, the class went to recess, but I stayed behind and hugged Tío again.

He started to cry again. "Tío, I'm sorry that I made you sad when I showed you my pulse."

"No te preocupes. Don't worry, Angel. I have been sad for a long time. It felt good to talk and share my feelings, like Miss Morris said."

27

"I loved hearing about how much fun you used to have. I hope someday that I can go to a place like Pulse and we can dance and have fun together."

"I would like that very much.
We should all feel safe
wherever we are.
We're all different, but still
part of one human family."

As Tío Luis said this,
I saw him smile.

Artist Credits

Ethan Long	Cover, 23, 32	ethanlong.com
Scott Donald	3	tsyklonstudio.com
Katrina Constantine	4, cityscape	kickingcones.com
Jacob Park	5	jacobkpark.com
Victor Davila	6	victordavila.com
Chelsey Austin	7	artofchelsey.com
Tara Tokarski	8, 22	taratokarskiillustrations.fineartstudioonline.com
Dawn Schreiner	9	dawnschreiner.com
Liz Von Villas	10,11	eawilliamson17@gmail.com
John Carmean	12	johncarmean.com
Stephanie Valderrama	13	simplysteph.co
Alexa Ponce	14, 15	alexaponcedesigns.com
Reina Castellanos	16	reinavsreina.com
Daniel Traynor	17, 28, 29	danieltraynor66.wixsite.com/illustrations
Gladys Jose	18, 19	gladysjose.com
Carlos X Diaz	20	carlosxdiazart@gmail.com
Hugo Giraud	21	hugogiraud.com
Shauna Lynn Panczyszyn	25	shaunalynn.com
Fernando Sosa	26	politicalsculptor.com
Kristen Pauline	27	kristenpauline.com
Matt Wilson	30	mswilson331@gmail.com
Anna McCambridge	31	annamccambridge.com

Director of Art and Layout - Ethan Long

Special Thanks to:
Bob Kodzis and Mac Baker

About the Orlando United Assistance Center

All profits from the sale of this book will be
donated to the Orlando United Assistance Center.

ouac

The Orlando United Assistance Center is a place offering support, resources, and hope for those impacted by the Pulse tragedy. A collaboration between the City of Orlando, Orange County Government, and Heart of Florida United Way, the OUAC connects individuals and families with community resources to assist with healing.

Learn more about the
Orlando United Assistance Center at
orlandounitedassistancecenter.org

From Joél Morales

"My life changed on June 12, 2016; when the world woke up to news of a mass shooting in a nightclub in Orlando - a place I would often visit and spend time with friends. Through my work and connections I found myself on the frontline after the tragedy working with those directly impacted and that work still continues.

I've learned that when community violence happens suddenly and without warning, youth and families have heightened fears that harm could come at any time. They begin to feel that the world they knew is now unsafe and terrifying. Collaborating on *My Tío's Pulse* has uplifted my spirits and aided me in my personal healing. This book can be used as a tool and an outlet to encourage everyone including children to talk about their feelings.

Our youth hold a special compassion not only for the communities they are a part of, but even those they aren't. They offer a love for each other that holds no barriers and affirms all identities."

In honor of the 49 lives lost in Pulse.

Joél Morales,
Orlando United Assistance Center

How To Help Your Child After a Tragedy

Things to Look Out For

Usually, anniversaries of a tragedy bring back emotions and thoughts that may have already settled. It is important to remember that children often "act out" how they feel instead of talking about it. Here are some common reactions to look for, especially when they were not there before:

- Losing interest in activities
- Prolonged fear of being alone
- Not wanting to close doors
- Problems sleeping
- Wetting the bed

- Withdrawal
- Excessive daydreaming
- Anger outbursts, aggressiveness
- Clumsiness
- Change in appetite

Changes are often signals children give out for us to pay closer attention. If these "signals" persist, please contact the Orlando United Assistance Center to obtain information about counseling for your children.

From **Kenny Tello**, LCSW, CAP, CCTP

"Children are often silent victims of tragedies. Sometimes we assume that they're too young to grieve, and that time and distractions will somehow make it ok for them. Nothing can be further from the truth. Children hurt and grieve just like everyone else, it just looks different.
Their experiences are as important and they need the space, time and words to walk through their grief.
This book was born out of the desire to help children find the words to describe an indescribable experience. To provide some light when reminders take them back to a dark place. And to help them find value and meaning in their experiences."

Kenny Tello, LCSW, CAP, CCTP

Things You Can Do

Here are some simple things you can do to help your children during this time.

Answer the questions. Years later, children may still have questions. It is often best to ask them first about what they know or what they think the answer is before providing them with our answers.

Give them words. As your children try to express their feelings, you can help them by using the characters from the movie "Inside Out" by Pixar or using "emojis."

Listen. Encourage them to talk to you and when they do, listen and validate their emotions. You don't have to fix it, you just have to be present with them in that space.

Hold them. Avoid the temptation to say "don't cry because it makes me sad to see you like this." Instead, hold them gently and let them cry for as long and as often as they need to.

Write it out. If they are old enough, have them write out their feelings. If not old enough, have them draw them. You can then ask them about what they want to do, whether they want to keep it, burn it, shred it, share with others, etc.

Include them in ceremonies or activities. You can have them play a small role such as lighting a candle, sharing a favorite memory, giving out food, etc. Author Alan Wolfelt says it best: "If they are old enough to love, they are old enough to mourn."

Create a memento. If appropriate, help children develop or select an item that brings a sense of safety and/or comfort. It could be something they could wear like a custom bracelet, necklace, a matching shirt, a keychain, or something they can put inside a stuffed animal.

From **Carolyn Capern** and **Greg Trujillo**

When Keith brought us his inspiration for a children's book to help parents talk to their kids about Pulse, we couldn't help but see it as an idea worth turning into reality. It's been an honor to see it come together, thanks to the talents of the creative and compassionate minds at work on every stage of the project.

Mayra Alvear, whose daughter, Amanda, lost her life at Pulse and who we met through the healing work of the Orlando United Assistance Center, told us that one of the most important things we can do to honor her daughter's memory is spread a message of love. In memory of our angels and in honor of our resilient survivors, let's all continue to invest in ideas that make the world a more beautiful and loving place.

Carolyn Capern & Greg Trujillo
Co-Owners, CTS Agency

From **Ethan Long**

"At 8 AM on the morning of Sunday, June 12th, 2016, I popped out of bed and walked up to the center of College Park, Orlando to sketch some of the local landmarks. Six hours earlier and 4.3 miles away, 49 people were killed and 53 more injured in the shootings at Pulse. This book is dedicated to all who lost their lives and the family and friends who have had to move forward through the grieving.

We understand it is a hard subject to discuss with kids, but maybe *My Tío's Pulse* will change that. Thank you, Keith, Carolyn and Greg for inviting me into this amazing collaboration."

Ethan Long
children's book author and illustrator

Special Thank You From the Author

When the *My Tío's Pulse* project started, I had no idea how much support the project (and I) would receive.

From the moment I shared the concept with Carolyn Capern, I've been overwhelmed with emotion as each individual who learned about it would not only ask "Why hasn't this been done already?!?", but go above and beyond to become a part of *My Tío's Pulse*. The energy and enthusiasm for the project has been incredible and I'm so grateful to so many for their help, love, and support.

As always, thank you to my family and friends for always being there for me and putting up with my insanity.

Thank you to all of the artists who have brought the book to life. It has been a pleasure working with all of you and so much thanks for your patience and energy throughout the process.

The following people have been instrumental in helping *My Tío's Pulse* become a reality and the project could not have been completed without them:

- Carolyn Capern (CTS Agency)
- Greg Trujillo (CTS Agency)
- Joél Morales (Orlando United Assistance Center)
- Kenny Tello, LCSW, CAP, CCTP (Orlando Health)
- Ethan Long (and the Orlando GIANT Illustrators)
- Blue Star (Come Out With Pride)
- Karen Brown (Come Out With Pride)
- Lynn and Lee DeScalzo (Fineline Printing & Graphics)

Of course a special thanks to you the readers, for using this book to help those who've been affected by Pulse and other tragedies. I hope that the work all of these incredible individuals have put into this project helps you and your loved ones heal and feel "safe" again.

Keith A. Newhouse

keithanewhouse.com

About NCG Cares

Newhouse Creative Group cares about our schools, children, and communities. That's why a major part of our business is about giving back. Through NCG Cares, we're partnering with others who want to make a difference in the lives of children. With programs like *My Tío's Pulse* and NCG Earn and Learn, we're "inspiring the readers and writers of today and tomorrow" and helping them succeed!

Visit NewhouseCreativeGroup.com for more books and other products from NCG Cares, AimHi Press, and the rest of the Newhouse Creative Group family!

Made in the USA
Middletown, DE
13 June 2019